SNOOPY ™

COWABUNGA!

Other *Peanuts* Kids' Collections

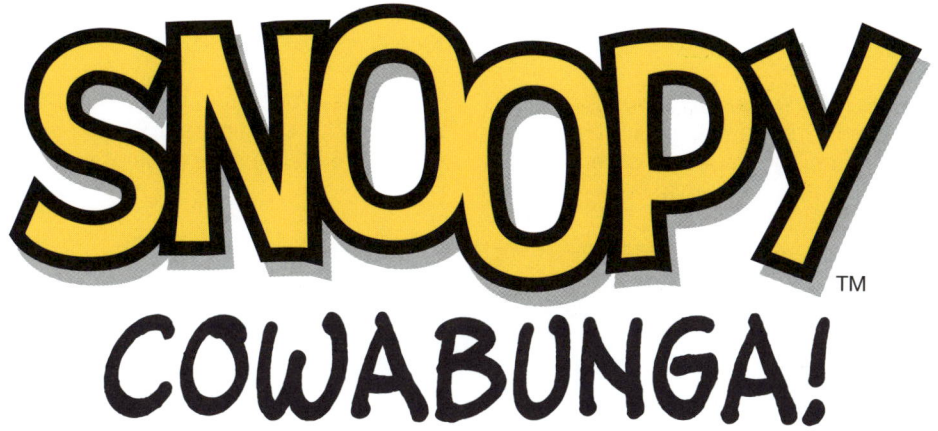

SNOOPY™
COWABUNGA!

A **PEANUTS**™ Collection

CHARLES M. SCHULZ

Andrews McMeel
PUBLISHING®

Peanuts is distributed internationally by Andrews McMeel Syndication.

Andrews McMeel Publishing
a division of Andrews McMeel Universal
1130 Walnut Street, Kansas City, Missouri 64106

www.andrewsmcmeel.com

www.peanuts.com

19 20 21 22 23 SDB 15 14 13 12 11 10

ISBN: 978-1-4494-5079-3

Library of Congress Control Number: 2013940278

Made by:
Shenzhen Donnelley Printing Company Ltd.
Address and location of manufacturer:
No. 47, Wuhe Nan Road, Bantian Ind. Zone,
Shenzhen China, 518129
10th Printing—4/8/19

ATTENTION: SCHOOLS AND BUSINESSES
Andrews McMeel books are available at quantity discounts with bulk purchase for educational, business, or sales promotional use. For information, please e-mail the Andrews McMeel Publishing Special Sales Department:
specialsales@amuniversal.com.

Why dogs are superior to cats.

They just are, and that's all there is to it!

SHORT AND TO THE POINT!

I FINALLY FOUND THAT BOOK I'VE BEEN WANTING TO GET YOU...

HOW NICE!

"DARWIN AND THE BEAGLE"

BIRDS HAVE SOME PECULIAR ATTRIBUTES...

WHICH CAN BE VERY HARD ON THE BRANCHES...

WHEN BIRDS FALL ASLEEP ON TREE BRANCHES, THEIR CLAWS AUTOMATICALLY TIGHTEN TO KEEP THEM FROM FALLING OFF...

OR SOMEONE'S NOSE!

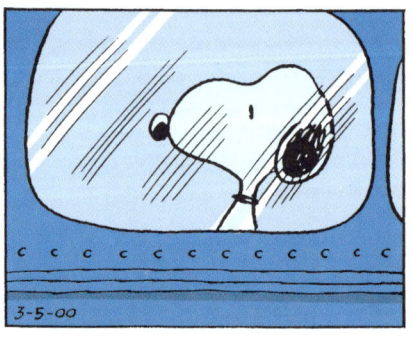

3-5-00

THAT'S THE TROUBLE WITH LIVING IN A QUIET NEIGHBORHOOD...

I HAVE TO TAKE A BUS ALL THE WAY DOWNTOWN WHEN I WANT TO CHASE CARS!

CHOMP
CHOMP
CHOMP

WOODSTOCK IS THE ONLY PERSON I KNOW WHO CAN BLOW HIS MIND ON BREAD CRUMBS...

"DEAR CONTRIBUTOR, YOUR STORY WAS TERRIBLE!"

"WE WOULD LIKE TO SEND IT BACK TO YOU, BUT YOU DID NOT INCLUDE RETURN POSTAGE"

" P.S. DON'T SEND THE RETURN POSTAGE NOW..."

3/31/00

"WE THREW YOUR STORY OUT THE WINDOW!"

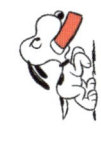

4-30-00

ACTUALLY, THE MAIN REASON I'M HERE IS TO REVIEW THE SHOW FOR OUR SCHOOL NEWSPAPER...

SCHULZ

5/9/00

YOU CAN'T BE A TENDERPAW FOREVER, YOU KNOW...

YOU HAVE TO WORK YOUR WAY UP... YOU ALSO HAVE TO EARN MERIT BADGES AND THINGS!

I KNOW THAT... I'M GOING TO WORK AND WORK UNTIL I'VE REACHED THE TOP....

BEAGLE SCOUT!!

HERE'S THE WORLD FAMOUS BEAGLE SCOUT SETTING OFF ON A HIKE..

HE TAKES WITH HIM ONLY THE BARE NECESSITIES...

EXTRA SOCKS, FIRST-AID KIT, A MAP, A COMPASS...

5/10/00

..AND LUNCH!

AN OBSERVANT SCOUT CAN LEARN A LOT ON A HIKE...

HE CAN LEARN ABOUT THE "WEB OF NATURE"

SUNLIGHT, AIR, PLANTS, WATER, SOIL, BIRDS, MICROORGANISMS....

ALL WORKING TOGETHER TO MAKE A BETTER LIFE FOR BEAGLES!

HERE'S THE WORLD-FAMOUS BEAGLE SCOUT ON A HIKE

GETTING OUT INTO THE OPEN LIKE THIS MAKES YOU LOOK AT LIFE DIFFERENTLY...

IT MAKES YOU REALIZE JUST HOW EASY IT IS TO BECOME...

..LOST!

5-7-00

SUDDENLY I FEEL VERY FAT!

SCHULZ

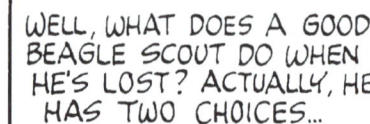

SNOOPY WENT ON A HIKE, AND NEVER CAME BACK... I WONDER IF HE'S LOST...

OF COURSE, HE'S LOST!

THAT STUPID BEAGLE COULDN'T FIND THE NOSE ON HIS FACE! HE COULDN'T FIND HIS HANDS IN HIS MITTENS! HE COULDN'T FIND THE EARS ON HIS HEAD!

5-16-00

I DON'T THINK HE'S THAT BAD... AFTER ALL, HE **IS** A BEAGLE SCOUT, YOU KNOW...

I THINK I'LL WAIT FOR THE MOON TO COME UP... I'VE HEARD THAT THE MOON ALWAYS POINTS TOWARD HOLLYWOOD...

I SEE SOMEONE!

IS IT A RESCUER? MAYBE IT'S SOMEONE COMING TO MUG ME! IT'S BAD ENOUGH BEING LOST WITHOUT GETTING MUGGED, TOO!

5-17-00

HE'S GETTING CLOSER! I'M TRAPPED! I'M DOOMED!!

HELLO! MY NAME IS LORETTA, AND I'M SELLING GIRL SCOUT COOKIES!

6/10/00

HE WHO LIVES BY THE POACH DIES BY THE POACH!

Kitten Kaboodle was a lazy cat. Actually, all cats are lazy.

6-13-00

Kitten Kaboodle was also ugly, stupid and completely useless.

But, let's face it, aren't all cats ugly, stupid and completely useless?

I LOVE WRITING ANTI-CAT STORIES!

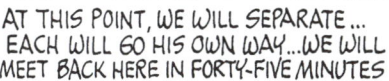

And so, once again, Kitten Kaboodle had to admit she had been outsmarted by a dog.

6-14-00

An ordinary dog at that.

DO YOU THINK THERE'S A MARKET FOR ANTI-CAT STORIES?

"PLAYBEAGLE" HAS BOUGHT THE WHOLE SERIES!

Secretly, Kitten Kaboodle wished she were a dog.

She was aware of the natural superiority of a dog, and it bothered her.

6-15-00

I THINK YOUR ANTI-CAT STORIES SHOW TOO MUCH PREJUDICE.. I THINK YOU'RE GOING TO MAKE A LOT OF ENEMIES...

NOT EVERYONE HATES CATS, YOU KNOW!

I FIND THAT HARD TO BELIEVE

After that, Kitten Kaboodle never again tried to match wits with a dog.

DO YOU THINK YOUR ANTI-CAT STORIES WILL EVER BE MADE INTO A TELEVISION SERIES?

I EXPECT TO HEAR FROM THREE NETWORKS... CBS, NBC AND ABC...

COLUMBIA BEAGLE SYSTEM, NATIONAL BEAGLE COMPANY AND THE AMERICAN BEAGLE COMPANY!

6-16-00

6-17-00

YOU KNOW THE CAT NEXT DOOR, DON'T YOU?

UNFORTUNATELY, I DO!

YOU KNOW WHAT I HEARD HE SAID?

I COULDN'T CARE LESS!

HE SAID IF HE FINDS OUT WHO'S BEEN WRITING THOSE ANTI-CAT STORIES, HE'S GOING TO JAM HIS TYPEWRITER DOWN HIS THROAT!

I SHOULD'VE HAD THAT POINT, AND I SHOULD'VE HAD THAT GAME AND I SHOULD'VE HAD THAT SET...

7-10-00

UNFORTUNATELY, WE'RE NOT PLAYING "SHOULD'VES"!

Edith had refused to marry him because he was too fat.

"Why don't you go on a diet?" suggested a friend. "You can't have your cake and Edith too!"

7-12-00

MMMMM!

IT'S EXCITING WHEN YOU'VE WRITTEN SOMETHING THAT YOU KNOW IS GOOD!

6-25-00

7-22-00

DROWNED IN A SEA OF STRING!

The curtain of night enveloped the fleeing lovers.

Though fiery trials had threatened, oceans of longing had kept them together.

Now, a new icicle of terror stabbed at the embroidery of their existence.

7-26-00

JOE METAPHOR!

7-02-00

INTERMISSION

THAT WAS A LONG FIRST ACT...DO YOU WANT TO WALK AROUND A BIT...MAYBE STRETCH OUR LEGS?

I COULD USE A DRINK OF WATER

HE PUTS ON A GOOD SHOW, DOESN'T HE? I'M VERY IMPRESSED...

THERE'S ONLY ONE THING HIS THEATER NEEDS...

A DRINKING FOUNTAIN!

ANYONE WHO WOULD SIT IN A TREE PRETENDING TO BE A VULTURE SHOULD GO TO SEE A PSYCHIATRIST!

SHE'S SO STUPID...

8-1-00

SHE SHOULD KNOW THAT VULTURES ALMOST NEVER GO TO SEE PSYCHIATRISTS!

SCHULZ

THERE IS NOTHING MORE TERRIFYING THAN THE SIGHT OF A VULTURE PERCHED IN A TREE WAITING FOR A VICTIM...

8-2-00

?

SCHULZ

SIGH!

44

8-3-00

SUDDENLY, I JUST FELT VERY VERY RIDICULOUS!

BEWARE OF THE DOG

8-4-00

A few thoughts concerning a lost love.

8-15-00

Rats!

I'VE SAT HERE NOW FOR SEVEN HOURS, AND NOT ONE PERSON HAS SAID A KIND WORD TO ME!

HELLO THERE, LITTLE FRIEND

RATS!

THERE GOES MY SPOT IN THE "GUINNESS BOOK OF WORLD RECORDS"!

8-21-00

3-19-00

YOU KNOW WHAT?

WHAT?

SIX HOURS IS A LONG TIME TO STAND HERE..

THAT'S TRUE

BUT WHERE ELSE ARE YOU GOING TO SEE "WAR AND PEACE" PERFORMED WITH HAND PUPPETS?

WOODSTOCK IS THE ONLY PERSON I KNOW WHO COULD GET CHASED FOR THREE BLOCKS BY AN ABALONE!

Gentlemen,

Enclosed is the manuscript of my new novel.

I know you are going to like it.

In the meantime, please send me some money so I can live it up.

SOMETIMES I THINK YOU MUST BE VERY NAIVE

8-25-00

NO ONE IS EVER GOING TO PAY YOU FOR THOSE DUMB STORIES YOU WRITE!

WAAH!!

AND CRYING WON'T HELP... PUBLISHERS VERY SELDOM PAY AUTHORS JUST TO KEEP THEM FROM CRYING...

WHAT'S WRONG WITH THOSE GUYS?

Joe Sportscar spent ten thousand dollars on a new twelve cylinder Eloquent.

9-1-00

"You think more of that car than you do of me," complained his wife.

"All you ever do these days," she said, "is wax Eloquent!"

OH, WOW!!!! HOW DO I DO IT?!

9/22/00

THIS IS A GREAT EXERCISE...

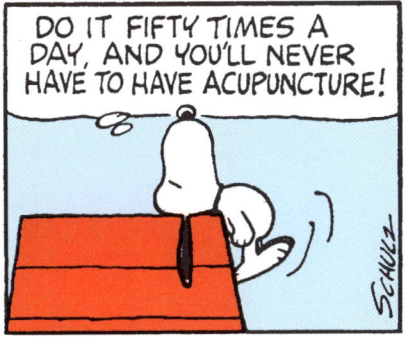

DO IT FIFTY TIMES A DAY, AND YOU'LL NEVER HAVE TO HAVE ACUPUNCTURE!

SCHULZ

9/23/00

WATCH IT, DOG!

IF YOU TOUCH THAT BLANKET, THE ODDS ARE A THOUSAND TO ONE THAT YOU WILL END UP WITH A BROKEN ARM!

I ALWAYS GO WITH THE ODDS

SCHULZ

LOOK, DOG, THIS IS A BRAND NEW PIANO...

10/17/00

IF THERE'S ONE THING IT DOESN'T NEED, IT'S A LOT OF CLAW MARKS!

HOW ABOUT A DISTRESSED FINISH?

HA!

10/21/00

I GOT 'IM NOW!

TWO GOOD SERVES AND A COUPLE OF BAD CALLS, AND I'M IN!

10/28/00

The

A GOOD WRITER WILL SOMETIMES SEARCH HOURS FOR JUST THE RIGHT WORD!

?

IT'S CALLED A "PUMPKIN"

???

TONIGHT IS HALLOWEEN... ALL THE PUMPKINS YOU SEE TONIGHT ARE FILLED WITH GHOSTS!

10/31/00

HELLO, CHUCK? TELL MY SKATING PRO I'M ENTERING A COMPETITION, AND I NEED A FEW LESSONS...

11/2/00

SKATING PRO? I DON'T KNOW ANY SKATING PRO...

C'MON, CHUCK, GET WITH IT! YOU GOT THE BEST ONE IN THE BUSINESS RIGHT THERE..

HERE'S THE WORLD-FAMOUS CRABBY SKATING PRO WALKING OVER TO THE RINK TO CHEW SOMEBODY OUT...

YOU SHOULD TRY ICE SKATING, MARCIE...

I HAVE WEAK ANKLES, SIR

THERE ISN'T SUCH A THING, MARCIE...

IT'S JUST A MATTER OF HAVING SKATES THAT FIT PROPERLY... MAYBE WHEN MY SKATING PRO GETS HERE, YOU COULD TRY A FEW LESSONS...

11/3/00

ROWF!

HE'S CRABBY, BUT HE'S A GOOD TEACHER!

11/4/00

WELL, PRO, WHAT DO YOU THINK?

BLEAH!!

THAT WAS A TEN-DOLLAR LESSON?

SNOOPY, LOOK AT THIS SKATING DRESS!

THAT STUPID MARCIE HAS RUINED EVERYTHING! WHAT AM I GOING TO DO?

WHEN A SKATER IS FEELING LOW, SHE SHOULD BE ABLE TO CRY ON HER PRO'S SHOULDER.. I CAN'T EVEN DO THAT....

11/15/00

YOU DON'T HAVE ANY SHOULDERS!!!

63

Once there were two mice who lived in a museum.

One evening after the museum had closed, the first mouse crawled into a huge suit of armor.

12/1/00

Before he knew it, he was lost. "Help!" he shouted to his friend.

"Help me make it through the knight!"

12/6/00

WOODSTOCK'S STORIES ALWAYS START OFF GOOD, BUT THEN THEY GET VERY SAD...

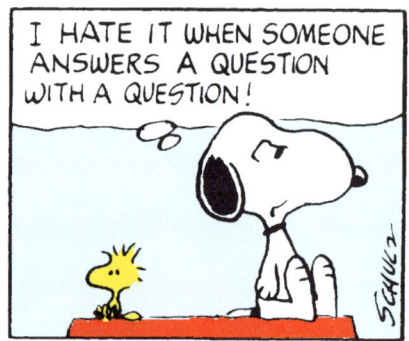

I WONDER WHAT WOULD HAPPEN IF I TRIED TO MAKE FRIENDS WITH THAT STUPID CAT NEXT DOOR...

I COULD SHOW HIM MY GOOD WILL BY EXTENDING MY PAW IN FRIENDSHIP...

12/12/00

BY GOLLY, I'LL DO IT!

SCHULZ

IT'S THE HOLIDAY SEASON, CAT!

IT'S TIME FOR YOU AND ME TO FORGET OUR DIFFERENCES! IT'S TIME TO BE FRIENDS...

12/13/00

SO HERE I AM EXTENDING TO YOU THE RIGHT HAND OF FELLOWSHIP...

SCHULZ

HERE COMES WOODSTOCK ON HIS NEW BICYCLE...

12/26/00

!!!

I HATE IT WHEN HE SAYS, "LOOK, NO WINGS!"

SCHULZ

12/27/00

Gentlemen,
        I ordered a toy bicycle for my sister's doll set.

It was supposed to be here by Christmas. Perhaps it was delivered to the wrong address.

Would you look into the matter, please?
        Thank you.

I REFUSE TO BE THE ONE WHO TELLS HIM!

SCHULZ

12/28/00

I ORDERED A TOY BICYCLE FOR YOUR DOLL SET, BUT IT NEVER CAME...

I HAVE A FEELING IT WAS PROBABLY DELIVERED TO THE WRONG ADDRESS...

WELL, I HOPE WHOEVER GOT IT, ENJOYS IT!!

WHEELIES, YET! GOOD GRIEF!

12/31/02

\|||\|||?

WHAT A STUPID QUESTION!

WHY WOULD I FORGET THE ROOT BEER AND THE OLIVES?

WHAT DO YOU DO WITH TWO FRIENDS WHO ARE HAVING A MISUNDERSTANDING?

1-9-01

STRAIGHTEN THEM OUT! SHOW 'EM WHERE THEY'VE GONE WRONG!! TELL 'EM TO SHAPE UP!!!

IS THAT GOOD PSYCHOLOGY?

IN STRICT MEDICAL TERMS, IT'S CALLED "BUTTING IN"!

I HAVE A SUGGESTION

DOESN'T EVERYONE?

WHY DON'T YOU TRY TO FIND OUT WHAT IT WAS THAT YOU BROKE AT WOODSTOCK'S PARTY?

1-10-01

MAYBE THAT WOULD BE THE FIRST STEP TOWARD YOUR RECONCILIATION..

I ALWAYS TRIP ON THAT FIRST STEP

THE WAR IS OVER, AND THE WORLD WAR I FLYING ACE IS HOME...NERVOUS AND RESTLESS, HE SEARCHES FOR SOMETHING TO DO...

GIRLS AND ROOT BEER ARE NOT THE ANSWER!

BARNSTORMING! THE QUEST FOR ADVENTURE LEADS HIM TO BARNSTORMING!!

STATE FAIRS CLAMOR FOR HIS ACT!

STUNT FLYING!

ADMI 10

THE CROWDS SCREAM WITH TERROR AS HE PERFORMS INCREDIBLE AERIAL ACROBATICS...

OOO!

AH!

WOW! GEE!

AND NOW, HERE'S THE WORLD WAR I FLYING ACE PERFORMING HIS MOST DANGEROUS STUNT...

9-3-00

WING WALKING!

SCHULZ

WE'LL GO OVER TO MY HOUSE...

WE'LL QUAFF A FEW ROOT BEERS, AND WE'LL SETTLE OUR DIFFERENCES LIKE CIVILIZED GENTLEMEN...

GULP GULP GULP

QUAFF QUAFF QUAFF

1-13-01

IT NEVER FAILS...THREE ROOT BEERS AND WOODSTOCK FALLS SOUND ASLEEP!

Z

"I INVITED YOU TO MY NEW YEAR'S PARTY BECAUSE YOU ARE MY FRIEND"

"THERE WAS SOMEONE ELSE AT THE PARTY THAT I WANTED YOU TO MEET"

"SHE'S THE CUTEST LITTLE BIRD I'VE EVER KNOWN, AND YOU MONOPOLIZED HER THE WHOLE EVENING.."

1-15-01

"IT BROKE MY HEART.....THAT'S WHY I SENT YOU A BILL FOR SIX DOLLARS.."

I SPOILED WOODSTOCK'S PARTY!

HE HAD INVITED THIS CUTE LITTLE BIRD THAT HE'S IN LOVE WITH, BUT HE NEVER GOT TO TALK WITH HER BECAUSE I TALKED WITH HER THE WHOLE EVENING!

1-16-01

SO HE SENT ME A BILL FOR SIX DOLLARS FOR A BROKEN HEART! OH, WOODSTOCK, MY LITTLE FRIEND OF FRIENDS...

DON'T YOU REALIZE THAT YOUR HEART IS WORTH MUCH MUCH MORE THAN SIX DOLLARS?!!

SIGH..

1-26-01

WOODSTOCK'S NEST ➡

NEXT NINE EXITS

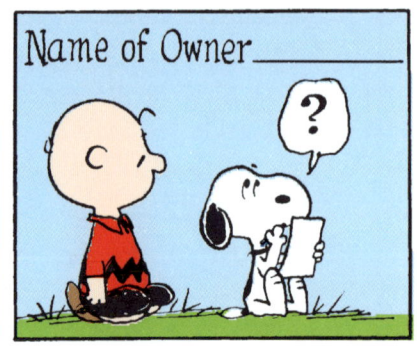

THIS IS THE GREAT NEW EXERCISE I'VE DEVELOPED...

YOU HAVE TO DO THIS FIFTY TIMES A DAY...

10-8-00

IT'S GOOD FOR YOUR NECK...

AND YOUR BACK...

AND YOUR LEGS...

WUMP!

BUT IT RUINS YOUR BODY...

91

I would like to nominate Snoopy for Neighborhood Dog of the Year because

3-9-01

he's kind of fuzzy.

He is truly a good dog.

type
type
type

He is also a loyal friend.

3-10-01

Therefore, I would like to recommend ol' banana nose for Neighborhood Dog of the Year.

HEE
HEE
HEE
HEE
HEE
HEE

ARGGH!

HERE'S THE WORLD FAMOUS BEAGLE SCOUT STARTING OFF ON A ROCK HUNTING EXPEDITION..

AH! HERE'S A NICE ONE...

OOOO! HERE'S A BEAUTY!

AH!

10-22-00

THIS IS YOUR ROCK COLLECTION? LET ME SEE...

BOY, WHAT A DUMB LOOKING ROCK COLLECTION! IT LOOKS LIKE YOU FOUND THEM ALL IN A DRIVEWAY!

NO ONE WOULD EVER BE INTERESTED IN A BUNCH OF ROCKS LIKE THAT..

NOT EVEN THEIR MOTHERS?

SCHULZ

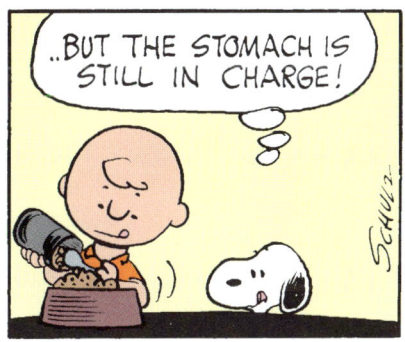

3-19-01

MOST BIRDS LAND BETWEEN THE LITTLE POINTY THINGS...

3-24-01

10-29-00

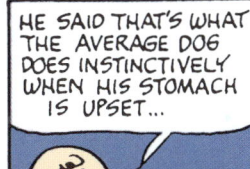

This is a story of Greed.

5-15-01

I'M GLAD TO SEE YOU'RE WRITING ABOUT GREED...

ONE OF THE SECRETS OF GOOD WRITING IS TO DEAL WITH REAL HUMAN EMOTIONS

Joe Greed was born in a small town in Colorado.

5-29-01

HE ADMITTED IT, AND I FORGAVE HIM...

BUT I STILL DON'T THINK A FRIEND SHOULD EAT THE HEAD OFF YOUR CHOCOLATE BUNNY!

11-12-00

CHEAP SHOT!
CHEAP SHOT!

ACTUALLY, IT WAS A GOOD
LEGAL CHECK, BUT YOU
NEVER WANT TO ADMIT IT!

7-10-01

I HATE SLEEPING IN WOODSTOCK'S GUEST ROOM!

SCHULZ

LET ME SEE...

7-14-01

I PROMISE NOT TO LAUGH!

BRACES!

SCHULZ

SO HERE WE GO ON A LITTLE PICNIC...

I BRING THE SALAD, THE SANDWICHES, THE PICKLES, THE POTATO CHIPS AND THE ROOT BEER...

7-19-01

WOODSTOCK BRINGS THE MARSHMALLOW!

7-21-01

THAT JUST DOESN'T WORK..

I HAVE TO SLEEP IN THE SAME DIRECTION THAT THE WORLD TURNS

Though her husband often went on business trips, she hated to be left alone.

"I've solved our problem," he said. "I've bought you a St. Bernard. Its name is Great Reluctance."

8-6-01

"Now, when I go away, you shall know that I am leaving you with Great Reluctance!"

She hit him with a waffle iron.

8-7-01

OVERHEAD SMASH!

COVER YOUR MOUTH! IT'S A DRAGONFLY!!

8-8-01

DRAGONFLIES SEW UP YOUR LIPS SO YOU CAN'T EAT, AND YOU STARVE TO DEATH!

WHEW!

THERE'S SOMETHING I THINK I SHOULD TELL YOU...

DRAGONFLIES DO NOT SEW UP YOUR LIPS SO YOU CAN'T EAT, AND YOU STARVE TO DEATH!

8-9-01

A LOT SHE KNOWS!

STOP COMPLAINING... IT'S NOT SUPPERTIME YET!

WOULD I LIE TO YOU?

WHEN IT'S SUPPERTIME, THE ROUND-HEADED KID WILL SHOW UP...JUST BE PATIENT!

SEE? HERE HE IS NOW.... RIGHT ON TIME!

12-10-00

CHOMP CHOMP CHOMP!

NOW, AREN'T YOU ASHAMED OF YOURSELF?

I HATE A STOMACH THAT ALWAYS HAS TO HAVE THE LAST WORD!

HERE'S JOE MOTOCROSS GOING OUT TO START HIS BIKE...

8-13-01

VAROOM!

RIP! RIP! RIP! RIP! RIP! RIP! POOOOOOOSHHH!

THE NEIGHBORS HATE ME!

8-14-01

HERE'S JOE MOTOCROSS CHECKING OUT THE COURSE...

WE GO AROUND THIS TURN, AND DOWN BETWEEN THOSE TWO TREES...

THEN WE GO UP THIS....

THEY'RE KIDDING!!

SNOOPY! WHY DON'T YOU COME INTO THE HOUSE, AND I'LL FEED YOU HERE? IT'S A LOT WARMER!

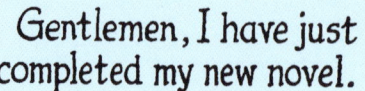

Gentlemen,

Well, another day has gone by and you still haven't come to pick up my novel for publication.

8/31/01

Just for that, I am going to offer it to another publisher.

Nyahh! Nyahh! Nyahh!

SCHULZ

I HOPE HE DOUBLE-FAULTS...

PLEASE DOUBLE-FAULT! DOUBLE-FAULT! DOUBLE-FAULT! DOUBLE-FAULT!

9/3/01

THAT WAS TOO BAD!

SCHULZ

TODAY FOR "SHOW AND TELL" I HAVE BROUGHT MY BROTHER'S DOG...

9/13/01

WHICH MAY TURN OUT TO BE THE BIGGEST MISTAKE OF MY LIFE!

9/14/01

THE DOG IS REGARDED AS THE FRIEND OF MAN...

THIS PARTICULAR BREED IS GENERALLY QUITE GENTLE AND THIS PARTICULAR DOG IS BOTH GENTLE AND INTELLIGENT...

ALTHOUGH HE DOES HAVE HIS FAULTS...

SUCH AS FLIRTING WITH THE GIRL IN THE FRONT ROW!!!

9/15/01

STUPID BEAGLE!

ALL BECAUSE OF YOU, I FAILED SHOW AN' TELL!

NOW, I'LL PROBABLY GET BAD GRADES ALL YEAR AND NEVER BE A GOOD STUDENT AND NOT GET INTO THE COLLEGE OF MY CHOICE!

SMAK!

POOR, SWEET BABY!

His wife had always hated his work.

9/18/01

"You'll never make any money growing toadstools," she complained.

"On the contrary," he declared. "My toadstool business is mushrooming!"

She creamed him with the electric toaster.

"Do you love me?" she asked.
"Of course," he said.

"Do you really love me?" she asked.
"Of course," he said.

10/15/01

"Do you really really love me?" she asked.
"No," he said.

"Do you love me?" she asked.
"Of course," he said.
So she asked no more.

SCHULZ

"Our love will last forever," he said.

"Oh, yes, yes, yes!" she cried.

10/17/01

"Forever being a relative term, however," he said.

She hit him with a ski pole.

SCHULZ

10/19/01

"CLOSE DANCING" IS COMING BACK!

10/20/01

YOU CAN'T SLEEP ON A COLD NOSE!

135

1/2/02

THE SNOW GODS HATE ME!

LOOK AT THAT!

DON'T YOU EVER WORRY ABOUT THAT STUPID BEAGLE, CHARLIE BROWN? JUST LOOK AT HIM! HE'S COVERED WITH SNOW!!

1/3/02

DON'T YOU EVER WORRY ABOUT HIM?

ACTUALLY, I'M FINE, BUT SOMEONE COULD SLIP ME A TOASTED ENGLISH MUFFIN IF HE WANTED TO..

ACTUALLY, WOODSTOCK PROBABLY SHOULDN'T HAVE A PAPER DELIVERED TO HIS HOME..

2/4/02

NEVER SHARE YOUR PAD WITH A RESTLESS BIRD!

2/9/02

WOODSTOCK WANTS TO FLY TO DISTANT HORIZONS BUT HE DOESN'T KNOW WHERE THEY ARE

SIGH

Dear Contributor,
We regret to inform you that your manuscript does not suit our present needs. The Editors

AUGH!

BAM!

5·6·01

CRASH

STOMP! STOMP!
STOMP! STOMP!

WHAM!

P.S. Don't take it out on your mailbox.

I SHOULD THINK YOU'D GET BORED JUST SITTING ON A DOGHOUSE ALL DAY..

2/11/02

ON THE CONTRARY..

WHO COULD GET BORED FLYING THE STAR SHIP "ENTERPRISE"?

THIS IS A LETTER TO MISS HELEN SWEETSTORY..

DEAR MISS SWEETSTORY... IT OCCURRED TO ME THAT NO ONE HAS EVER WRITTEN THE STORY OF YOUR LIFE...I SHOULD LIKE TO DO SO...

THEREFORE, I PLAN TO VISIT YOU FOR A FEW WEEKS TO BECOME ACQUAINTED, AND TO GATHER INFORMATION ABOUT YOUR LIFE AND CAREER...

2/15/02

P.S. BEFORE I ARRIVE, PLEASE LOCK UP YOUR CATS!

MISS SWEETSTORY ANSWERED MY LETTER!

"DEAR FRIEND, THANK YOU FOR WRITING... SINCERELY, HELEN SWEETSTORY"

SHE WANTS ME TO VISIT HER!

THIS IS A **FORM** LETTER!

2/16/02

MISS SWEETSTORY HAS INVITED ME TO HER HOME, AND WANTS ME TO WRITE THE STORY OF HER LIFE!

THIS IS A FORM LETTER!!

SOME PEOPLE JUST CAN'T READ BETWEEN THE LINES!

YOU'RE GOING TO VISIT MISS SWEETSTORY?

I'M GOING TO INTERVIEW HER, AND WRITE HER BIOGRAPHY

YOU DON'T EVEN KNOW WHERE SHE LIVES!

I'M SURE SHE LIVES IN A WHITE VINE-COVERED COTTAGE WITH ROSE BUSHES, A PICKET FENCE AND A WILLOW TREE...

I'LL KNOW IT WHEN I SEE IT!

2/18/02

YOUR DOG HAS NO RIGHT TO WALK OFF AND LEAVE YOU, CHARLIE BROWN!

YOU FEED HIM, AND YOU GIVE HIM A HOME...IN RETURN, IT'S HIS JOB TO GUARD YOUR PROPERTY, AND BE YOUR FRIEND! THE TROUBLE WITH YOU IS YOU DON'T KNOW HOW TO RAISE A DOG, CHARLIE BROWN!

2/25/02

HAVE YOU EVER RAISED A DOG?

OF COURSE NOT!! I WOULDN'T EVEN OWN A DOG!

ANOTHER UNMARRIED MARRIAGE COUNSELOR.. ❄ SIGH ❄

WHAT'S THAT? WHAT DID YOU SAY?

THERE IT IS! A VINE-COVERED COTTAGE WITH ROSE BUSHES, A WILLOW TREE AND A PICKET FENCE!

2/26/02

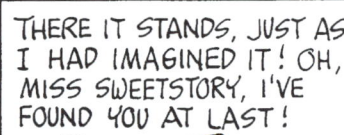

THERE IT STANDS, JUST AS I HAD IMAGINED IT! OH, MISS SWEETSTORY, I'VE FOUND YOU AT LAST!

WHEN SHE ANSWERS THE DOOR, I'LL REMOVE MY DOG DISH AS IF IT WERE A HAT, I'LL BOW AND IN A VERY DIGNIFIED MANNER I'LL SAY,...

"HI, SWEETIE!"

A Biography of Helen Sweetstory

YOU'RE BACK! WHEN DID YOU GET BACK? DID YOU MEET MISS SWEETSTORY? DID YOU INTERVIEW HER? WHAT IS SHE LIKE?

DID SHE ANSWER ALL YOUR QUESTIONS? WAS SHE NICE?

DOES SHE REALLY LIVE IN A VINE-COVERED COTTAGE?

I MAY HAVE TO RENT A STUDIO DOWNTOWN..

Helen Sweetstory was born on a small farm on April 5, 1950.

I THINK I'LL SKIP ALL THE STUFF ABOUT HER PARENTS AND GRANDPARENTS...THAT'S ALWAYS KIND OF BORING...

I'LL ALSO SKIP ALL THE STUFF ABOUT HER STUPID CHILDHOOD... I'LL GO RIGHT TO WHERE THE ACTION BEGAN...

It was raining the night of her high-school prom.

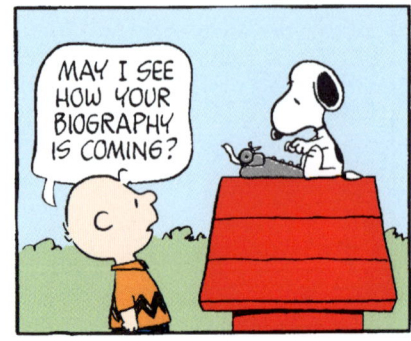

SPRING MUST BE NEAR..

3/14/02

WOODSTOCK JUST RETURNED FROM THE OTHER END OF THE DOGHOUSE

I JUST READ SOMETHING THAT AMAZED ME..

DID YOU KNOW THAT WE SPEND ONE-THIRD OF OUR LIVES SLEEPING?

3/15/02

SOME TYPES SPEND NINE-TENTHS OF THEIR LIVES SLEEPING...

I'M GOING TO PRETEND I DIDN'T HEAR THAT!

167

RAIN!

IT HELPS THINGS TO GROW... IT FILLS UP THE LAKES AND OCEANS SO THE FISH CAN SWIM AROUND AND IT GIVES US ALL SOMETHING TO DRINK..

WOODSTOCK DOESN'T CARE WHAT IT IS AS LONG AS HE UNDERSTANDS IT

SO YOUR SISTER THREW YOU OUT OF THE HOUSE..

YES, I'M LIVING HERE IN THE DORM WITH JOE COOL

IS IT COMFORTABLE? HOW'S THE FOOD? WHERE DO YOU EAT?

I DON'T KNOW.. I SUPPOSE WE EAT IN THE CAMPUS CAFETERIA

5/13/02

NO WAY! JOE COOL ALWAYS SENDS OUT FOR A PIZZA!

5/14/02

♥ HI, ♥ SWEETIE!

HI, JOE...WHO'S YOUR FRIEND WITH THE BLANKET?

THAT'S A GOOD QUESTION..

OUR DORM GETS ALL THE STRANGE ONES!

5/21/02

WHAT I DON'T UNDERSTAND IS WHY YOUR MOTHER WOULD ALLOW LUCY TO THROW YOU OUT OF THE HOUSE...

MOM ISN'T HOME...SHE WENT TO THE HOSPITAL YESTERDAY

!

IS SHE ALL RIGHT?

I DON'T KNOW.. NOBODY EVER TELLS ME ANYTHING...

A NEW BABY BROTHER?!! BUT I JUST GOT RID OF THE OLD ONE !!!

A NEW BABY BROTHER! I CAN'T BELIEVE IT!

5/22/02

YOU MIGHT AS WELL COME BACK IN... I CAN'T FIGHT THE WHOLE WORLD

WHAT DO YOU MEAN BY THAT?

DAD JUST CALLED FROM THE HOSPITAL..WE HAVE A NEW BABY BROTHER!

A NEW BABY BROTHER!?

I THROW ONE OUT, AND ANOTHER COMES IN! YOU CAN'T SHOVEL WATER WITH A PITCHFORK

177

7/15/01

Now is the time for all foxes to jump over the lazy dog.

6/4/02

SOMEHOW, THAT DOESN'T SEEM QUITE RIGHT...

6/5/02

WHAT A GREAT TITLE FOR MY NEW BOOK...

"THINGS I'VE LEARNED AFTER IT WAS TOO LATE"

Things I've Learned After It Was Too Late

6/6/02

Never argue with the cat next door. He's always right

Things I've Learned After It was Too late.

A whole stack of memories will never equal one little hope.

6/8/02

I KIND OF LIKE THAT

8/27/02

SIGH

WHY DO PEOPLE ALWAYS HAVE TO TELL YOU WHAT THEY DREAMED LAST NIGHT?

KLUNK!

8/31/02

THAT'S WHAT IS CALLED "COMING IN OFF THE BENCH"

SMAK!

POMPON GIRLS CAN'T RESIST A SUPERSTAR!

STOMP!

RAH?

BONK!

WOODSTOCK HAS DIFFICULTY RECOVERING FUMBLES...

THAT STUPID WOODSTOCK... HE LOST HIS BOOK WITH ALL OUR SECRET PLAYS!

9/6/02

TWENTY THOUSAND LAPS AROUND THE FIELD!

WHAT A LOUSY BREAK!

NO WONDER COACHES GO CRAZY...

9/7/02

FIRST GAME OF THE SEASON, AND WHAT HAPPENS?

MY MIDDLE LINEBACKER GETS HIS HEAD CAUGHT IN HIS LOCKER!

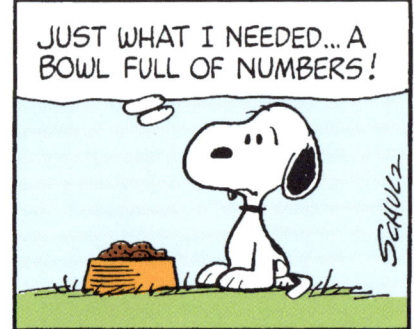

9/16/02

9/21/02

"FEAR OF FALLING LEAVES."... WHEN WE GET HOME, I'LL HAVE TO LOOK THAT ONE UP...

10-20-02

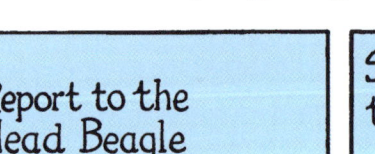

11/26/02

WOODSTOCK FEELS THAT EATING BREAD CRUMBS IS KIND OF DEGRADING...

IT SNOWED LAST NIGHT..

NOW, I CAN'T SEE A THING... SUDDENLY I'M SHUT OFF FROM THE WORLD AND ALL ITS PROBLEMS

12/17/02

LET'S HEAR IT FOR THE SNOW!!

In addition to all these great Snoopy cartoons, here are some cool activities and fun facts for you. Thanks to our friends at the Charles M. Schulz Museum and Research Center in Santa Rosa, California, for letting us share these with you!

Make a Recycled Bird Feeder for Woodstock and His Friends

MATERIALS: empty plastic water bottle, Popsicle stick, birdseed, scissors, tape

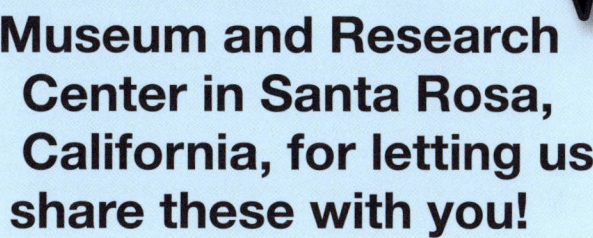

INSTRUCTIONS:

1 Cut an opening in one side of the bottle and fill it with birdseed.

2 Decorate the bottle with paint or markers. Tape a Popsicle stick to the opening for a bird perch.

3 Tie a ribbon on top of the bottle for a hanger and hang it outside for birds to enjoy.

Make Snoopy's Dog House

MATERIALS: an 8.5 x 11 inch piece of paper, scissors, tracing paper

Start with the piece of paper. The best paper to use is colored on BOTH sides, but in the illustrations, the side of the sheet that will end up INSIDE the doghouse is white, just to make it easier to see the folds. Match corners and edges carefully and crease well.

1 Bring bottom edge to top. Crease flat.

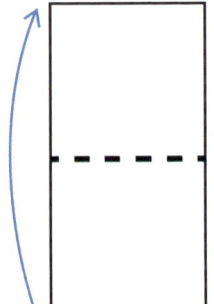

2 Rotate so open edge is at the bottom. Bring bottom edge of top layer to the top. Crease flat.

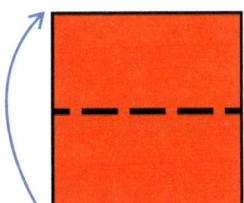

3 Turn over and repeat on other side, then rotate so open edges face down.

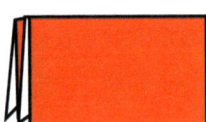

4 Lift the bottom edge of one side and make a fold upwards, along an imaginary line about one-half inch below the top fold.

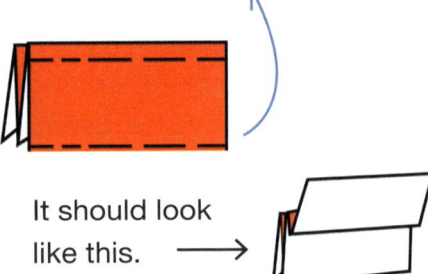

It should look like this. ⟶

5 Turn over. Bring corners of second side up to meet corners of folded side. When pressed flat, it will crease in the right place.

It will look like this:

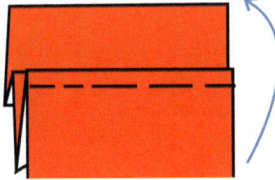

Now rotate:

6 Lay it flat, and turn down (dog-ear) the corners of the middle fold, as squarely as you can. Crease well! Turn over and repeat.

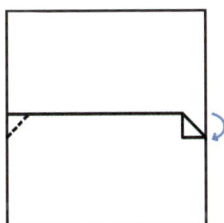

Hint: Try for *square corners* like this:

Not like this:

7 UNFOLD the corners, and poke them INSIDE the fold, along the creases you just made. Press flat.

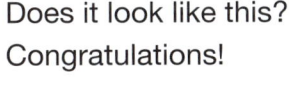

Does it look like this? Congratulations!

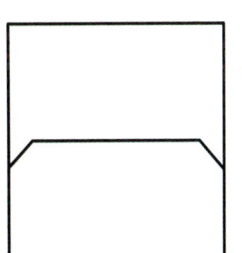

8 Fold back each edge of the top layer by opening the little corners and creasing a fold parallel to the vertical sides. Fold both edges, then turn over and repeat on other side.

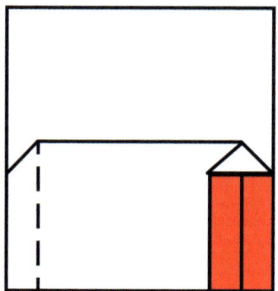

It should look like this:

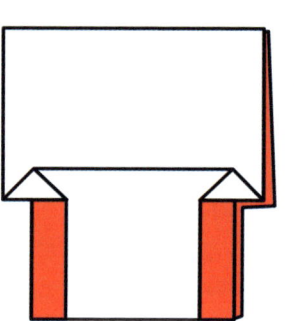

9 Re-fold the TOP of the house in the other direction, putting all your work INSIDE. Yay! A house! Now we just have to make the roof edges slant.

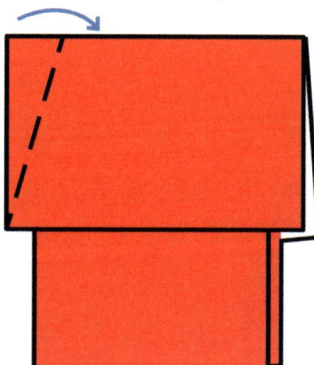

10 Fold a narrow slanted edge on each side, as shown. Crease well, unfold, and poke inside. Flatten.

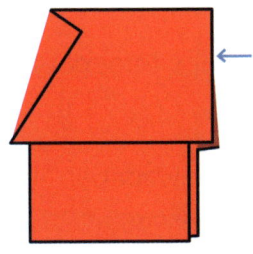

Leave room for Snoopy!

11 Open the ends a little and apply tape.

Trace the Snoopy art below, color it in, cut it out, and put Snoopy on his roof!

Charles M. Schulz and *Peanuts* Fun Facts

🐾 Charles Schulz drew 17,897 comic strips throughout his career.

🐾 Schulz was first published in Ripley's newspaper feature *Believe It or Not* in 1937. He was fifteen years old and the drawing was of the family dog.

🐾 From birth, comics played a large role in Schulz's life. At just two days old, an uncle nicknamed Schulz "Sparky" after the horse Spark Plug from the *Barney Google* comic strip. And that's what he was called for the rest of his life.

🐾 In a bit of foreshadowing, Schulz's kindergarten teacher told him, "Someday, Charles, you're going to be an artist."

🐾 Growing up, Schulz had a black-and-white dog that later became the inspiration for Snoopy—the same dog that Schulz drew for Ripley's *Believe It or Not*. The dog's name was Spike.

🐾 Charles Schulz earned a star on the Hollywood Walk of Fame in 1996.

Learn How Comics Can Reflect Life

MATERIALS: blank piece of paper, pencil, markers or colored pencils

1 Make four blank cartoon panels, all the same size, on the piece of paper.

2 Look at the example below to see how Charles Schulz used his own life in his strips—even painful experiences like that of loss—and turned them into strips. Think of something that has happened to you at home or school that had a big impact on you.

3 Once you have decided on a story you want to tell, draw it in four panels. Remember, it should have a beginning, a middle, and an end.

An example from Schulz's life:

In 1966, a fire destroyed Schulz's Sebastopol studio. He translated his feelings into a strip about Snoopy's doghouse catching fire:

Make a Snoopy Finger Puppet

MATERIALS: an 8.5 x 11 piece of paper, black construction paper, red or pink construction paper, scissors, tape, black marker

1 Fold paper into thirds, lengthwise.

2 Fold the paper in half by bringing one of the open ends to the other and creasing a fold in the middle.

3 Bring one of the open ends up to the middle and crease flat.

4 Turn the paper over.

5 Bring the second open end up to the middle and crease flat.

6 The finished folded square should look like an "M" or "W" when placed on its side on a flat surface.

7 Hold the square with the open ends facing you.

8 Use your thumb and index finger to gently pinch the folded points toward each other so the open ends open up.

9 Pull the two inside pages together.

10 Place a piece of tape over the middle of the inside pages.

11 Put your index finger and middle finger inside one of the pockets you have created.

12. Put your thumb inside the pocket below.

13. Close the puppet mouth by bringing your thumb to your index and middle finger. Open the puppet mouth by opening your fingers.

14. Cut out two ears from black construction paper and glue them to the face of your Snoopy.

15. Cut out one tongue from red or pink construction paper and glue it inside Snoopy's mouth.

16. Use a black marker to give Snoopy eyes.

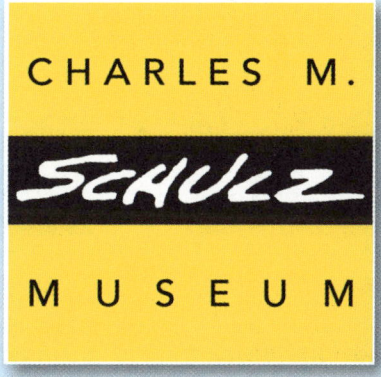

It should look like this!

A round-headed boy named Charlie Brown, a security blanket, and a five-cent psychiatrist—just some of the classics you will find when you visit the largest collection of *Peanuts* artwork in the world. Laugh

CHARLES M.
Schulz
MUSEUM

at Schulz's original comic strips, learn about the art of cartooning, and Schulz's role in its development, watch documentaries and animated *Peanuts* specials in the theater, and draw your own cartoons in the hands-on education room. The Museum features changing exhibitions, a re-creation of Schulz's art studio, outdoor gardens, holiday workshops. and special events. Take a virtual tour of the Museum at schulzmuseum.org!

Check out more *Peanuts* kids' collections from Andrews McMeel Publishing.

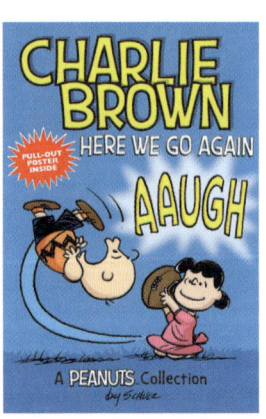